To all peace-loving,
truth-seeking,
and altruistic people.

www.enchantedlion.com

First edition published in 2022 by Enchanted Lion Books
248 Creamer Street, Studio 4, Brooklyn, New York 11231

Text and illustrations copyright © 2022 Nahid Kazemi
Editors: Claudia Bedrick and Emilie Robert Wong
Book design: Lawrence Kim

ISBN 978-1-59270-352-4
Printed in China by RR Donnelley Asia Printing Solutions Ltd.
First Printing

Nahid Kazemi

Shahrzad &
the Angry King

Enchanted Lion Books
NEW YORK

Once upon a time,
there was a girl named Shahrzad,
who fell in love with stories
long before she could read or write.

She found stories everywhere—
in peoples' faces and gestures,
in shops and cafes, and throughout
the city's streets.

Shahrzad was
always listening.

Always waiting for another story.

She listened to every story she came upon, with a smile from ear to ear.

She thought hard about each story she heard,
and what it might mean, no matter where she was.

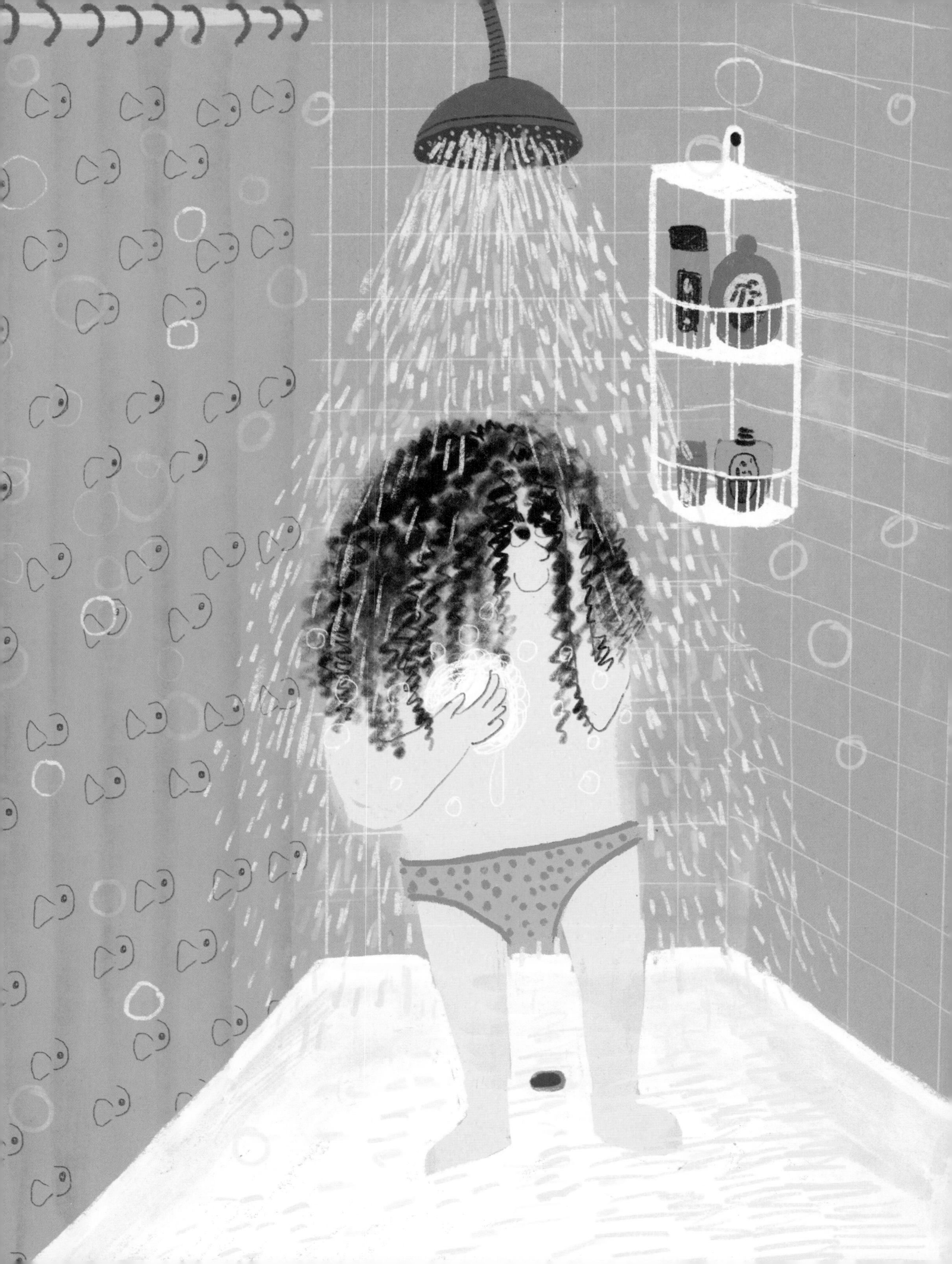

And because she was always listening to stories,
she was able to regale others with them, too.

When she was alone in her room, she would write down
the things she had seen or heard to better understand people.

One day, when she saw a boy
alone in the park looking sad,
she naturally had to find out
what was going on.

Shahrzad learned that the boy and
his family had come from far away.

"It started with the king," the boy told her.
"Well, with the king's wife."

"She was gentle and wise,
and the king loved her very much.
Soon, their baby would be born."

"The king was kind and fair,"
the boy continued, "and the town
was peaceful and happy."

"Then the queen got sick, and none of the doctors were able to save her or the baby."

"The poor king," said Shahrzad. "He lost his family all at once."

The boy nodded. "I never saw anyone sadder. But after a while, he grew angry. He stormed around his palace, clenching his teeth and pulling his beard. His shouting made the walls shake."

"Why was the king so mad?" Shahrzad asked.

"My parents say it's because he couldn't stand seeing other people happy."

Shahrzad thought she understood, and how hard it must be to feel so alone.

"Then he started to rewrite
the laws," said the boy. "First,
he banned parties and dancing.
Then, laughter became a crime.
Next, he banned sports and games,
and weekends. After, things got
even worse. With no rest or play,
people grew angry and mean."

The boy sighed. "The king has been this way for years now.
My parents say we can never go home."

The next day, Shahrzad couldn't stop thinking
about the boy, his city, and the king.

In a toy store, Shahrzad found some crowns and put one on
to see how it might feel to be a king.

When she found a large toy plane, she began
to imagine she was on it. She closed her eyes.
A few seconds later, she felt it taking off.

Shahrzad was piloting a plane! She sped across cities
and countries to reach the land from where the boy
had come. She wanted to help him. To do so, she
knew she would have to tell the king stories unlike
any he had ever heard.

So it was that Shahrzad arrived in the kingdom of the angry king.
It was completely still and silent. Shahrzad wondered if anger didn't
destroy stories somehow.

Everything felt strange and eerie, but Shahrzad
was determined to set things right and headed for
the imposing palace.

In the silence, she couldn't tell if the guards were real or statues.

But that changed when
the king saw Shahrzad and
bellowed: "Who are you?"

The tower swayed with fury.

"My name is Shahrzad, and
I've come to tell you a story."

The king glared down at her.
"A story? What kind of story?"

"The one about the angriest king
in the world."

Shahrzad saw the king's face redden.

"How dare you!" the king bellowed again.
"I'm the angriest king in the world!"

Shahrzad kept her voice calm. "You don't
look like the angriest king in the world."

"Is that so?" seethed the angry king.

"Well, for starters, the angriest king doesn't have a beard. He ripped it out ages ago."

The king touched his beard. It felt a little patchy.

"And he's toothless. All his teeth shattered because he clenched them so hard."

The king rubbed his jaw. His molars ached more than usual.

"Your king sounds ridiculous," said the angry king. "He cannot be the angriest king in the world."

"Why not?" Shahrzad asked.

"I bet his shouts don't shake his palace," the king argued.

"Of course not. He yelled so much that his palace collapsed years ago."

"Your king has no beard, no teeth, and no palace?" roared the angry king. "Well, then, he's no king at all, and he's no better than a fool!"

A crack appeared in the tower wall.

The king gasped. He would prove he wasn't like that other king—that he could maintain his power and be angry at the same time. The king stomped over to his desk to write his newest, meanest law yet.

When he finished, it was late, and all of the townspeople were asleep. Eager to put his great power on display, he decided he would wait until morning to introduce his cruel measures.

But by dawn, Shahrzad was back.

"Your highness, would you like to hear more about the angriest king in the world?"

He didn't know why, but the angry king did want to hear more. "I suppose the law can wait," he grumbled.

Shahrzad began again, and she talked until night fell. The king thought about yelling at her to go away, but he didn't want to destroy his palace. So Shahrzad remained, telling stories day after day.

And every night, she fell into a deep, dreamless sleep.

Each new day, her story began
where the last one had ended.

Shahrzad felt that the king was thinking
about her stories. When no one was around,
when there was no crown, or throne,
or glittery clothes. When he was just himself.

As for Shahrzad,
she kept thinking about
the boy, his city, and the
king, and all of the stories
she still needed to tell.

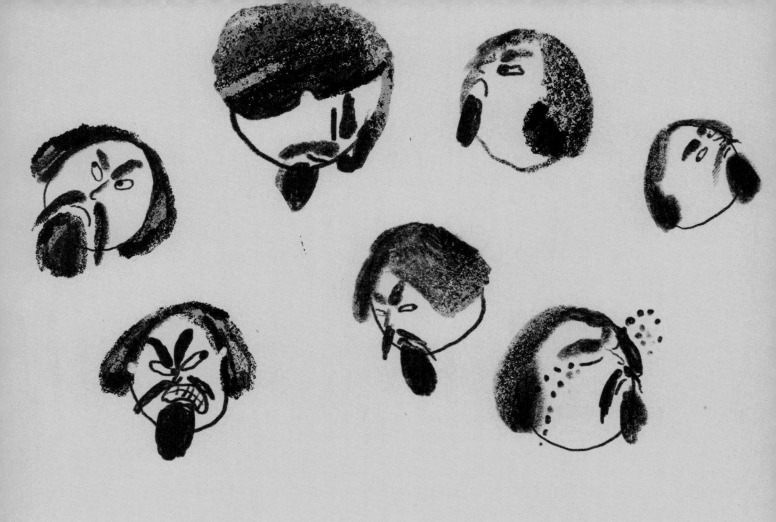

Some of her stories
made the king furious,
some made him sad,
some made him laugh,
and some made him cry.

Some were about people in lands ruled by angry kings.
These told of fear, sadness, death, and the loss of family and home.

Others were about people in lands ruled by happy kings.
These told of kindness, community, and of gathering
in parks that gave enjoyment to all.

One thousand and one nights passed.
Or maybe it was just ten, or a hundred,
or a hundred and one. Whatever the case,
the king's beard had grown bushier than ever.

Shahrzad knew it was time for her last story.

"Once upon a time, there was a boy who lived in a peaceful, happy town," she said. "Then the king's wife got sick, and everything changed."

She told him the story of his own kingdom,
of its weary parents and silent children.

When she finished, the king, who had been completely still
and had listened to every word, started up from his chair
and hurried away.

Shahrzad heard him shouting as he stormed off.

She hung her head. She had failed.

Shahrzad went outside to see what the king would do next.
People were coming to hear the news from far and wide.

But to Shahrzad's astonishment,
the king was not shouting angrily.
He was making an announcement,
declaring that he would revoke
each of his cruel laws.

Then he did something amazing.

"Thank you, Shahrzad," he said, "for helping
me to see that even though I can't bring
my own family back, I can create a kingdom
where everyone has the chance to be
as happy as I once was."

The children were the first to respond. Laughter and dancing filled the streets.

Shahrzad was dancing, too,
but when she opened her eyes,
she found herself back in the
toy shop.

When she was back in her room again, Shahrzad thought
about all she had experienced in the kingdom of the angry king,
and she decided that she would look for the boy the next day.
She wanted to tell him about the king and how he had changed.

And one day, she thought, *all of this will make a good story, too.*